THE SOUND OF ONE MONKEY

33 Zen Stories to Embrace Mindfulness, Quiet the Mind, and Find Peace in Simplicity & Meditation

Zen Tales

Book 3

KAI TSUKIMI

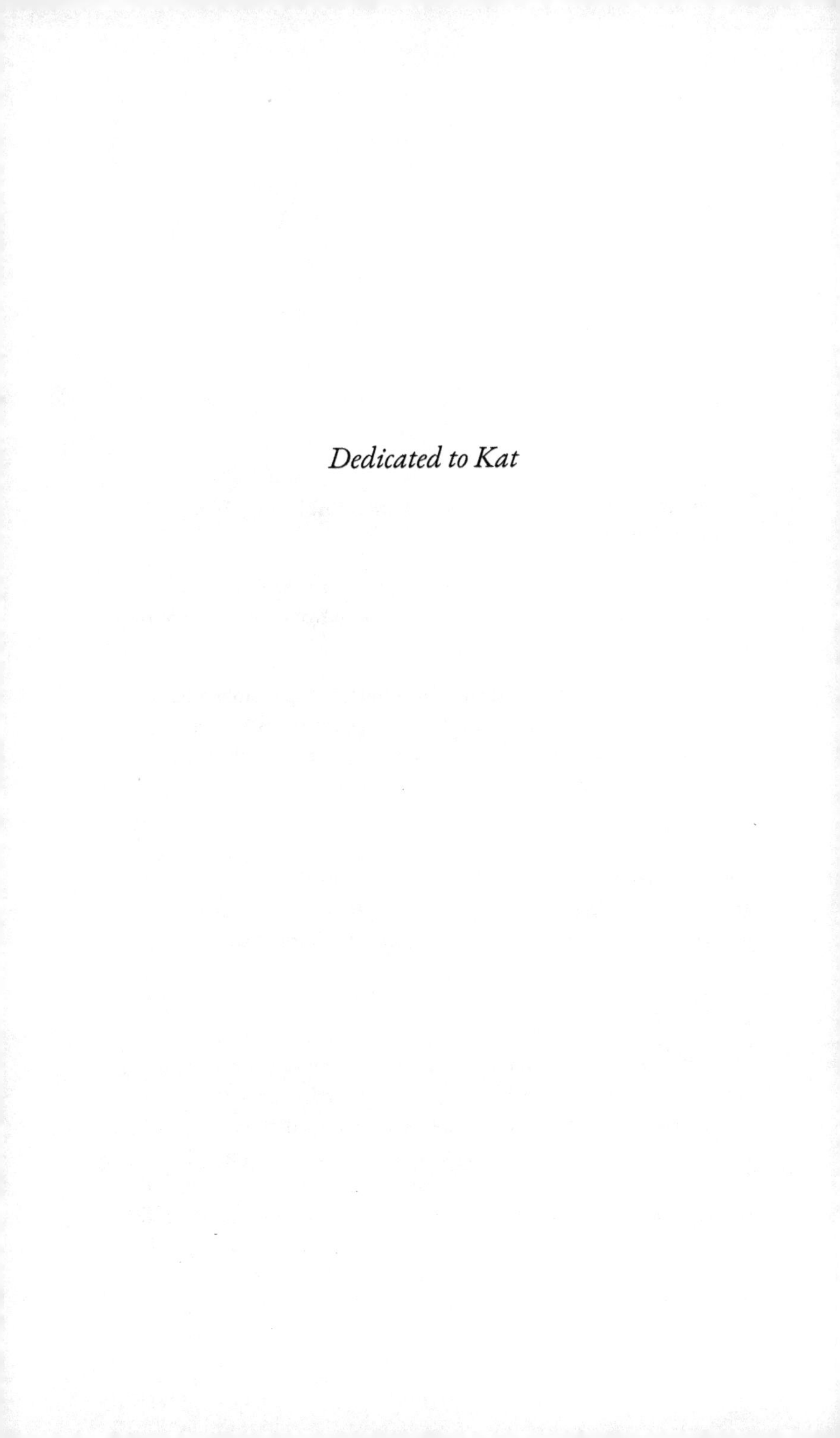

Dedicated to Kat

A book can shift your perspective, but a ritual can transform your life. As a thank-you for reading, I'd like to offer you our exclusive *Zen Clarity Kit*; designed to help you clear your mind, refocus, and make Zen teachings a part of your daily routine.

What's Inside the Kit?

✓ **The Zen Morning Ritual Guide**   A simple daily practice to anchor your mind in stillness.

✓ **A 5-Minute Audio Meditation** – Gently guide yourself into a state of clarity and focus.

✓ **Zen Minimalism Wallpapers** – Subtle reminders to cultivate presence throughout your day.

>> Scan the QR Code or click here
to download your free gift <<

Table of Contents

Introduction

What Is Zen?

If you ask ten Zen masters what Zen is, you'll get ten different answers—and none of them will satisfy you.

One might say it's the sound of bamboo in the wind.

Another might hit you with a stick.

Another might ask you where your thoughts go when you stop thinking.

The more you search for a definition, the more it slips through your fingers. Zen isn't a belief. It's not a technique. It isn't even something you "get."

It's what's already here—before the question.

It's the silence between thoughts, the feeling before the answer, the pause between one breath and the next.

And in this book, it takes the shape of a monkey.

Why a Monkey?

Because if Zen ever had a voice, it might sound like a monkey yelling from a tree.

The monkey is clever. Loud. Curious. It wants to figure everything out and do it fast. It interrupts meditation with questions, turns silence into performance, and makes everything a game of winning or losing. If you've ever tried to sit still and think of nothing, only to think about thinking of nothing—you've already met the monkey.

In Buddhist tradition, the "monkey mind" is restlessness itself—leaping, grasping, always unsatisfied. But this monkey? He's something more. He's got jokes. Opinions. A sense of style. He talks, argues, even insists he's right. He's the voice that doesn't stop... until something quieter finally does.

In this book, the monkey might be a trickster. A teacher. Or your own mind, dressed in a tail and grinning.

He might make you laugh. Or drive you mad. Or both.

That's the monkey's way.

What Are Zen Stories?

They're not stories in the usual sense. They're glimpses.

Small, strange moments meant to unstick you from your usual patterns of thought. They rarely explain themselves. They never arrive when you expect. They appear mid-step, mid-sentence, mid-life—and if you're lucky, they leave something behind.

A question. A feeling. A silence.

The Sound of One Monkey is a collection of 33 poetic Zen stories that follow a young monk and a mischievous monkey on a long journey toward a distant temple—and toward something wordless.

Some stories are surreal. Others are quiet and warm. Many are both. But none of them offer the kind of clarity you can hold. They invite you to notice the moments in between.

To watch your own monkey.

To see what happens when you stop answering him.

How to Use This Book

There is no right way to read it.

You can begin at the beginning, or start anywhere at all. You can read a single story and set the book down for a month. Or read three in one breath, laughing at how the monkey reminds you of... well, you.

At the end of each story, you'll find a few soft questions. They're not there to explain the stories. Just to deepen the quiet they leave behind.

This isn't a book of teachings. It's a book of echoes.

And sometimes, the quietest ones come from the loudest places.

So breathe. Listen.

Watch what rises. Watch what falls away.

And if you catch yourself trying to "understand," smile.

The monkey's still talking.

— Kai

PART I

The Monk and The Monkey

When the student is ready, the teacher will appear. When the student is truly ready... the teacher will disappear.

Lao Tzu

1
___

THE MONKEY WHO SPOKE FIRST

THE YOUNG MONK HAD TAKEN ONLY THREE steps beyond the monastery gate when he heard it.

"Well, it's about time," said a voice from the banyan tree. "I was beginning to think you'd never leave."

The monk froze. He looked left, then right, then up—and there, perched on a crooked limb like a sleepy guardian, was a small monkey with a smug grin and a half-eaten fig in its paw.

"I beg your pardon?" the monk said cautiously.

"You're pardoned," the monkey replied. "Now. Enlightenment, yes? Big temple at the end of the road. All very mysterious. Let's go."

The monk blinked. "You can talk."

"You can walk," said the monkey. "Should we stand here marveling at each other's miracles all day, or shall we begin?"

The monk hesitated. His training had prepared him for solitude, for silence, for watching clouds drift across empty sky. It had not prepared him for a monkey with impeccable timing and irritating confidence.

"Are you... a sign?" he asked, hopefully.

"Of what?"

"Of anything."

The monkey leapt down, landed without sound, and tossed the fig pit into a bush.

"I'm just a monkey. You're just a monk. The road is just a road. But between the two of us, one of us is going to get lost."

The monk opened his mouth to protest, but the monkey was already walking—tail high, stride casual, as if the path had been waiting for *him*.

And somehow, the monk followed.

He told himself it was out of curiosity. Or caution. Or to ensure the monkey didn't steal his lunch. But the truth was quieter, more difficult to name.

They walked in silence for a while.

"Do you have a name?" the monk finally asked.

"Of course."

The monk waited.

The monkey didn't answer.

**What part of you is the monkey
—and what part is the monk?**

そ

2

———

THE MEAL MADE OF AIR

THE STALL LOOKED ABANDONED, EXCEPT FOR the smell of something impossible.

No fire, no pots, no steam. Just four crooked stools and an old woman humming like she had a full orchestra behind her.

"I'm hungry," the monk admitted.

"You're fortunate, then," said the monkey, puffing out its chest. "This is the finest dining establishment on this path. Possibly in this lifetime."

The monk glanced at the empty counter. "There's no food."

The monkey tapped its nose. "Exactly."

The woman looked up. "One serving of the rarest kind of nourishment?"

"Yes, please," said the monkey, before the monk could protest. It turned to the monk. "Give her your coin."

"My last one?"

"Do you plan to carry it into enlightenment?"

Reluctantly, the monk placed the coin on the wooden plank. The woman pocketed it and poured absolutely nothing into a small wooden bowl. She passed it to the monkey with reverence.

The monkey inhaled. "Ahhh. Essence of sky, hint of mountain breeze, aged twelve seasons. Smell that?"

The monk sniffed. It smelled like bowl.

"Now," said the monkey, "eat."

The monk stared into the emptiness. Slowly, with all the solemnity of a tea ceremony, he lifted the bowl to his lips and pretended to sip.

The monkey watched him approvingly.

"Delicate, isn't it? Fills you up in places you didn't know were empty."

The monk nodded, trying to look wise. His stomach growled audibly.

The monkey burped.

They walked on.

After a while, the monk said, "I still feel hungry."

The monkey shrugged. "Then clearly, you didn't taste it properly."

What have you dismissed as "nothing" that might've been quietly nourishing you all along?

3

THE LEAF THAT REFUSED TO FALL

"That one," said the monkey, mid-chew. "That leaf right there. It'll never fall."

The monk looked up. A single yellow leaf clung to the end of a bare branch, fluttering faintly.

"All things fall," said the monk.

"Not that one."

The monk smiled. "Shall we bet?"

The monkey grinned wider. "Absolutely. If it falls, I'll carry your pack for the rest of the day. If it doesn't, you owe me your sandals."

The monk glanced at his sandals, worn but reliable. "Deal."

And so they waited.

The wind stirred. The branch trembled. The leaf danced, but did not let go.

Hour by hour, the monk kept vigil. The monkey lay on its back, whistling, occasionally tossing pebbles at nearby trees.

Night came. The monk refused to sleep.

"Go on," yawned the monkey, curled in a nest of leaves. "You can't catch it falling if your eyes are closed."

The monk stayed awake, blinking through moonlight, eyes fixed on the stubborn sliver of yellow.

By morning, his limbs ached. His thoughts were tangled vines.

The monkey stretched, scratched, and looked up.

"Still there?"

The monk nodded slowly.

The monkey shrugged. "Or maybe it fell while you blinked. Who's to say?"

The monk squinted. The leaf looked... familiar. Was it the same one? Had it moved? Was there even a leaf at all?

He looked down at his sandals, then up at the monkey, who was already reaching for them with a grin.

"I'll carry the pack," said the monk.

What are you holding onto so tightly that you no longer see it clearly?

13

4

THE SACRED STICK

THEY FOUND IT BESIDE A STREAM—A GNARLED stick, worn smooth on one end, bent like a question mark on the other.

The monkey picked it up reverently, dusted it off with exaggerated care, and held it out to the monk like a sword being passed between kings.

"This," the monkey said solemnly, "once belonged to a mountain hermit who tamed tigers with a whisper. He carved sutras into bark and silence into stone. He spoke only with this stick."

The monk blinked. "He spoke... with the stick?"

"Every thump was a teaching," said the monkey, tapping it three times on the ground. "Now, it's yours."

The monk hesitated. "Why me?"

"You're walking to the place where people stop walking," said the monkey. "You'll need something sacred for that."

So the monk took it.

He walked with it tucked into his robe belt, like a hidden truth. When he rested, he held it across his knees. When he rose, he tapped it once on the ground.

That night, he slept under a banyan tree, dreaming of tigers who bowed.

In the morning, he awoke to a child giggling nearby.

The stick was in the sand.

The child was using it to draw large, lopsided circles. Around and around. Then a spiral. Then nothing at all.

"Stop!" the monk snapped.

The child froze, wide-eyed.

"That's not a toy," the monk said, snatching it up. "It's sacred."

The child nodded silently and backed away.

The monk stared at the stick in his hands. It was smeared with sand and traced with a faint crack near the curve. He brushed it off, but something clung.

He sat down.

He looked at the lines the child had drawn. A circle. A spiral. A line that went nowhere.

Slowly, he placed the stick beside him—not on his lap, not across his knees. Just down to his side.

And the monkey, perched in a tree above, whispered, "Looks like it still speaks."

When have you held something so carefully that you forgot its purpose—and what changed when you let it be shared?

5

———

THE ROAD TO NOWHERE NEW

"I KNOW A BETTER WAY," THE MONKEY declared, already stepping off the path.

The monk glanced at the worn footpath stretching ahead. "To where?"

"To where you're going, of course," said the monkey. "Faster. Fewer blisters. More enlightenment per step."

The monk hesitated. "And how do you know where I'm going?"

The monkey waved a paw. "You're a monk. You're *always* going to some higher place. Trust me."

So they turned off the path and into the woods.

The shortcut was not exactly a path. It was more of a suggestion: narrow, twisting, cluttered with roots and riddles. They passed a bent tree whose trunk resembled a bowing man. Then a creaking bridge over a dry creek. Then a field where the grass leaned left.

After an hour, they passed the same bent tree.

The monk stopped. "We've been here."

"Similar trees," said the monkey. "Nature has themes."

Another hour. The same bridge. The same leaning grass.

"This is the same field," the monk said.

"Is it?" said the monkey, plucking a wildflower and tucking it behind its ear. "Or is it the same *feeling* in a different place?"

The monk frowned but said nothing. He walked faster.

They continued through the day. Each turn felt slightly familiar, like a song the monk couldn't quite remember.

At sunset, the trees thinned—and the main trail reappeared ahead.

The monk stopped.

They were back at the trailhead.

Exactly where they'd begun that morning.

The monkey stood beside him, gazing at the sky as if seeing it for the first time.

"Well," it said, "maybe the world's round."

The monk looked at the setting sun. Then down at his feet. Then at the monkey's face—unbothered, unsurprised, entirely at ease.

He sighed.

And kept walking.

**When have you mistaken movement for progress—
and what did you notice when you returned to
where you started?**

6

———

THE STORY HE COULDN'T FINISH

IT WAS NEAR DUSK WHEN THEY REACHED THE inn—lanterns swaying gently on crooked hooks, walls leaning like tired elders, the sign above the door too faded to read.

"No prices," noted the monk, peering at the empty menu board.

"Exactly," said the monkey. "A place of mystery. And trust. My kind of place."

The monk hesitated on the threshold.

"Quick choices show clarity," the monkey added, strolling inside.

So the monk followed, chose a modest room, and said nothing.

He slept soundly—dreamless, for once.

But in the morning, a firm knock woke him.

A woman stood at the door, arms crossed, hair braided like a crown of thorns.

"That'll be one story," she said.

The monk blinked. "Pardon?"

"One night's stay. Payment's a story."

He rubbed his eyes. "What kind of story?"

"Any kind," she said. "But it must be yours."

The monk sat on the edge of the straw mattress, breath catching somewhere between curiosity and dread.

"Well," he began slowly, "there was once a monk and... a monkey."

The monkey, who had been watching from the window ledge, grinned.

The woman nodded. "Go on."

The monk opened his mouth.

Nothing came.

His thoughts slid like pebbles in water—fragments of temples, footsteps, laughter, leaves that didn't fall, bowls filled with air. But none of it felt like a story. None of it had an end.

"I—" he started again, then faltered.

The woman waited a moment longer. Then she turned, walking away without a word.

The monkey hopped down beside him. "You know, most people don't realize they're in the middle of the story until it's too late."

The monk looked down at his hands.

Then out the window, where the trail was already beginning to disappear into morning fog.

If someone asked for your story as payment, what truth would you offer—and what might still be unfolding as you speak?

7

_____

THE BELL THAT RANG TOO SOON

"Do you think snails get bored?" the monkey asked.

The monk didn't answer right away. He was watching a hawk circle above the ridge.

"I mean, they don't _do_ anything," the monkey went on. "Just slime and glide. No drama."

And that's when it came—a low, distant toll.

The monkey froze mid-step, ears twitching.

"That's it," it hissed. "We're late."

"Late for what?" the monk asked.

"For the ceremony. The offering. The opening of the temple gates. Pick any sacred thing you like—we've missed it."

"But we don't even know—"

"Run!" the monkey barked, already sprinting down the path.

The monk followed, heart pounding. He ducked under branches, stumbled through brambles, leapt over streams. Mud clung to his robe like second thoughts. A thorn tore his sleeve. Still, the bell echoed—two, three more times.

He ran harder.

They reached the village at dusk, breathless.

Empty.

The streets were lined with closed shutters. No music. No incense. No people.

Just a single bell hanging in the plaza. Swaying gently in the breeze, clinking against itself with no rhythm, no ritual. No hand to strike it.

The monk stepped closer.

It was cracked.

Not in half. Just enough to never ring quite the same way twice.

The monkey wandered over, scratched its head, and said nothing.

The monk sat down on the stone beneath it, breathing heavily. He looked at his torn robe. His scraped palms. His blistered feet.

Above him, the bell tilted slightly, caught by a shift in the wind. It clinked again—softly this time.

Like a whisper.

Or a laugh.

What have you been rushing toward, only to find that what you feared missing was never quite what you thought?

8

THE MAP MADE OF INK AND IMAGINATION

"DID YOU KNOW," SAID THE MONKEY, CHEWING on a reed, "that some maps are drawn by dreams?"

The monk arched a brow. "That sounds... unreliable."

"Only if you don't dream correctly."

They were resting beneath a crooked tree, the kind that leans just far enough to make you think it might fall, but never does. The monkey was sprawled out, belly up, sketching something in the dirt with a sharp twig.

"There," it said at last, stepping back like an artist unveiling a masterpiece. "The better way."

The monk peered down. The drawing looked like a snake had fought a spider and lost.

"What is it?"

"A map."

"To where?"

"Forward."

The monk frowned. "It doesn't resemble the trail."

"Of course not," said the monkey. "This one's faster, stranger, and contains exactly three fewer regrets."

The monk hesitated. His feet were tired. His thoughts, more so.

So he followed.

The path wasn't marked—just impressions in the grass, the occasional footprint that might've belonged to the monkey or someone else entirely. Soon the trees began to change: their bark patterned like eyes, their leaves whispering as if passing secrets.

The rocks hummed—not songs, exactly, but tones that pulsed in the gut.

"Is this real?" the monk whispered.

The monkey didn't answer. It was whistling something tuneless, tail flicking like a metronome.

They passed a tree that wept clear sap onto a stone shaped like a sleeping face.

Then another, wrapped in a vine that pulsed with breath.

The monk stopped. "We're not on the map anymore."

The monkey looked back, blinked once, and said, "Weren't we never?"

By the time they returned to the main trail, the sky had shifted slightly. Colors more saturated. Air a little thinner.

The monk turned to look behind him.

There was no path.

Just trees.

Just wind.

Just a monkey, already walking ahead.

When have you followed an uncertain path—and how did you know whether it was a detour or exactly where you needed to go?

PART II

The World of Noises

Words are but the shadow of actions.

Master Linji

9

———

THE ROPE THAT REMEMBERS NAMES

THE MARKET APPEARED LIKE A MIRAGE—WOVEN awnings fluttering in the heat, tables overflowing with objects both strange and shining, voices weaving over each other like vines.

The monkey was immediately at home.

"Ooooh, trinkets!" it cried, darting from stall to stall. "Is it too early to buy enlightenment? Or do I need exact change?"

The monk walked more slowly, eyes catching glimpses: a jar of bottled shadows, a lute strung with silence, a wheel that spun but didn't move.

Then they saw the bracelet stall.

Dozens of small rope bracelets, each tied around a wooden peg. Each one bore a small paper tag with a name handwritten in faded ink.

Hope.

Fear.

Echo.

Midnight.

Breath.

Regret.

Home.

The vendor was ancient, folded in on himself like an unused fan. He didn't speak at first—just held out a bowl.

The monkey reached in without hesitation.

It pulled out a red bracelet with gold thread woven through. The tag read: *Victory.*

"Well, obviously," said the monkey, slipping it on. "This one knows who's boss."

The monk hesitated.

"Go on," said the monkey. "Pick one. Or are you afraid of who you'll be?"

The monk reached in.

His fingers brushed several cords. Then one curled around his wrist on its own.

He lifted it out. The bracelet was plain, frayed at the edges, soft with wear. Its tag was blank.

"No name?" asked the monk.

The vendor smiled for the first time.

"Not yet."

The monkey snorted. "Defective. You should get a refund."

They left the market, walking until the crowds faded and the sky stretched wide.

That night, after the fire had burned low, the monk sat cross-legged with the bracelet in his palm.

The monkey was asleep, snoring quietly, one paw draped dramatically over its face.

In the hush of the hour, the bracelet gave a tiny sound.

A hum.

Faint as memory.

Soft as breath.

And then, silence again.

Can you trust something before you understand it —and are you willing to let its meaning reveal itself over time?

10

THE BOY WHO HEARD NOTHING

THEY PASSED THROUGH A FLAT STRETCH OF land where the wind spoke louder than the trees. No villages. No signs. Just a boy, sitting in the dust at the side of the road, drawing spirals with his finger.

The monkey spotted him first.

"Aha! A witness to our greatness," it declared, puffing up its chest. "Watch this."

It bounded over.

"Boy!" the monkey called. "You there! What's your favorite fruit? Be honest. I can tell if you lie."

The boy didn't move.

The monkey tried again. "Do you know any jokes? I'll go first. What walks on four legs in the morning, two at noon, and none after enlightenment?"

Still no reply.

"Is he deaf?" the monkey whispered to the monk, scandalized. "Or just rude?"

The monk said nothing. He was watching the boy's hands, which had stopped tracing spirals and were now patting the ground, rhythmically, like he was feeling for something hidden beneath the earth.

The wind kicked up.

A tumbleweed scuttled past.

The monkey leaned in, frowning. "I think he's ignoring me."

Still no answer.

The monk knelt beside the boy, but didn't speak. He simply placed a hand gently on the dirt beside the child's.

The boy looked at him.

And then, after a long moment, he said:

"Sometimes I pretend I'm a donkey because they get better dreams."

And with that, he stood, brushed off his trousers, and walked away—slowly, as if listening for something else entirely.

The monkey opened its mouth. Closed it.

Then turned to the monk. "What does that *mean?*"

But the monk was still kneeling in the dust, smiling slightly, as if he'd heard the punchline to a joke that hadn't been told yet.

Can you sit with someone else's silence without trying to fill it—and what might emerge if you do?

11

THE TREE THAT SAID UP

The path split without warning.

One trail curving left into a forest of thick pine, the other sloping right toward a valley painted gold by the late afternoon sun.

The monkey froze mid-step, eyes narrowing. "Ah. A classic test."

The monk said nothing, but paused to drink from his flask.

The monkey climbed a nearby stump and struck a pose. "To the left: mystery, shadow, probably some ancient trial by moss. To the right: beauty, light, perhaps a scenic regret or two."

The monk looked between them.

"I vote right," said the monkey. "You look pale. And frankly, I deserve a nice view."

The monk looked around—and noticed a tree. Crooked and knotted, older than the others, its bark split like old laughter.

Carved into it, faint but deliberate: *UP.*

The monk tilted his head.

Above, balanced on a high branch, was a blue jay.

It tilted its head too. Then it took flight—north, over neither path.

The monk adjusted his robe and began walking—not left, not right, but forward and slightly uphill, following the bird's line.

The monkey called after him, indignant. "That's not a *path*! That's shrubbery!"

The monk kept walking.

The monkey pouted for exactly three steps, then scampered after him. "Fine. But if this ends in thorns, I'm blaming the bird."

Somewhere ahead, the blue jay landed on another tree.

And waited.

When faced with clear options, have you ever

chosen a direction that wasn't offered—and what guided you there?

12

———

THE MASTER WHO LAUGHED TOO LOUD

By late afternoon, the sun had pressed its weight into the backs of their necks, and the dust clung to their tongues like regret. Even the monkey stopped talking—mostly.

"Water," it wheezed. "Liquid enlightenment. We need it."

They spotted a stone hut by the edge of a hill, smoke rising in lazy loops. Outside sat an old man in layered robes, his face half-hidden beneath a tilted straw hat.

The monk bowed. "Excuse me, master. Is there water nearby?"

The man looked up.

Then burst into laughter.

"HOH! HOH! HOH!"

Loud. Unapologetic. It echoed down the hill and startled a nearby goat into running sideways.

The monk waited.

The monkey blinked.

"Excuse me," the monk tried again. "We've been walking a long—"

"HOH! HOH! HOH!" the man roared again, slapping his knee with a hand that seemed to have forgotten time.

The monkey stared. Then mimicked him.

"HOH! HOH! HOH!" it squawked, doubling over dramatically. "Look! I'm enlightened now!"

The old master said nothing more. Just kept laughing, slowly, until it faded into a wheeze and then a hum and then silence.

They left without water.

That night, lying on the earth, throat dry and limbs aching, the monk watched the stars.

One blinked in a pattern that reminded him of the goat's sideways sprint.

And for no reason at all, a giggle escaped him.

Not a big one. Just enough.

The monkey peeked over. "What's so funny?"

The monk didn't answer.

When was the last time you let yourself laugh without knowing why—and what did it loosen in you?

13

THE TEMPLE MADE OF SALT

They heard it before they saw it—the hush of waves, the slow breathing of the sea.

And then, like a mirage folding itself upright, the temple rose from the sand: white, angular, glistening in the sun.

A lone gatekeeper sat cross-legged by the entrance, gnawing lazily on seaweed.

"This place looks expensive," the monkey muttered.

The monk stepped forward. "May we enter?"

The gatekeeper squinted at them. "First, you taste it."

"Excuse me?" said the monkey.

The gatekeeper thumped a hand against the outer wall. "Lick."

The monkey hesitated. The monk, without pause, leaned forward and pressed his tongue to the wall.

Salt.

Sharp, pure, electric.

The monkey sniffed, then followed suit.

"Ohh," it whispered. "That's... oddly satisfying."

"The whole temple is made of it," the gatekeeper said. "But only until tomorrow."

"The tide?" asked the monk.

The gatekeeper nodded. "One more high wave, and it's gone. Built every month. Dissolves every month."

"That's absurd," said the monkey. "Beautiful things shouldn't just vanish."

"It always comes back," the gatekeeper shrugged.

But the monkey was already gathering driftwood, stacking seaweed, dragging rocks—trying to build a barrier.

"We can save it!" it shouted. "Just need more time, more walls, maybe some umbrellas!"

The monk wandered the temple instead. Room by room, he tasted walls. Some were sweeter, others bitter. One made his eyes water.

The monkey, covered in sand, returned with a palm leaf and a bucket.

"Help me," it demanded. "We can preserve the sacred."

But the monk just stood there, brushing salt from his lips.

"It was never ours," he said.

And that night, the tide came.

What beauty in your life are you trying to preserve, even though it's meant to dissolve?

14

***

THE ONE WHO CARRIED HER

THE RIVER HAD OVERRUN ITS BANKS, SLOW AND swollen from last week's storms. The crossing stones were buried. The current, though lazy, pulled with a silent promise.

She stood at the edge—robes soaked to the knee, a pack on her back, sandals in hand. She looked like someone who had walked a long way without much hope left.

"Looks like she's stuck," said the monkey.

The monk said nothing.

They stepped closer.

The woman turned, bowed. "I need to reach the other side."

"There's no bridge," the monkey said. "And you're not exactly a swimmer."

She said nothing. Just stared at the far shore.

The monk removed his sandals, tightened his belt, and gestured for her to climb on his back.

She did.

He waded slowly into the water. The current pressed against, but he kept his balance. The monkey hopped from rock to rock beside them, tail twitching nervously.

On the other side, the monk set the woman down. She bowed again. "Thank you."

Then she walked on.

The monkey watched her go, arms crossed.

They resumed walking.

After half an hour, the monkey exploded.

"You're not even going to talk about it?! We have *rules*, you know. Vows. Boundaries. You don't just carry someone like that."

The monk kept walking.

"She didn't even say anything interesting! What if she was a trick? A distraction? A—"

"I put her down at the river," the monk said quietly.

He didn't look back.

But the monkey did.

As if expecting to see her still there—carried now by something else entirely.

What weight are you still carrying, even though you've already set it down?

15

———

THE LANTERN HUNG UPSIDE DOWN

"IF I EVER START A VILLAGE," THE MONKEY announced, "everyone will walk backward for balance and hang their shoes from trees."

The monk didn't answer.

Not because it wasn't strange, but because they'd just stepped into a square lit by dozens of red lanterns... all hanging upside down.

The monkey blinked. "Wait. They've stolen my idea."

Hundreds of them. Big, small, round, crescent-shaped— suspended by their bases, flames flickering where tassels should be. The light curled upward, shadows bent unnaturally, as if gravity had been rewritten.

The monk stood still, caught in the quiet hum beneath the music.

The monkey scowled. "They're doing it wrong."

It darted ahead, leapt onto a table, then a post, then the lowest lantern. With great effort, it flipped it upright.

The crowd didn't cheer. Didn't move.

The music continued. The lights pulsed. No one said a word.

"This one too," muttered the monkey, climbing higher, reaching for another.

The monk glanced around. The villagers all stood watching, but not the monkey.

Then came the *roar*.

A raw, guttural sound that tore the music in half.

A single figure stepped forward from behind a curtain—an old master, dressed not in robes but in ash, his arms streaked with soot. His mouth was still open from the shout.

The monkey froze mid-climb, paw on a lantern's edge.

No one moved.

Then, as if remembering itself, the monkey slowly climbed down.

They walked out together, feet silent on the stone.

When they reached the edge of the trees, the monkey finally whispered, "They were upside down."

The monk said nothing.

When have you tried to fix something that wasn't broken—and who were you fixing it for?

16

THE VILLAGE THAT WAITED FOR SILENCE

THE MONKEY'S SANDAL HAD FALLEN APART during the last day.

By the time they reached the next village, it was flapping wildly with every step—*flap, flap, flap*—like an indecisive drumbeat.

"I need a new pair," the monkey declared. "Something stylish. Preferably with bells."

The monk gave a small nod. He was thinking of his own feet—blistered and sore.

The village seemed normal at first: tidy homes, a well in the center, shaded stalls selling fruit and thread. But something was missing.

No one spoke.

Not a whisper. Not a laugh. Not even the bargaining tones of coin-measured words.

The monk gestured politely to a vendor. Smiled. Bowed.

The vendor pointed toward a wooden board nailed to a post near the well.

Carved deep into the grain were the words:

When the bell rings, words may walk again.

The monkey read it twice. Then groaned.

"Oh no. Not another ritual. Not another... waiting-for-the-bell-before-you-buy-sandals village."

It marched up to a young girl, pointed at its feet, made exaggerated stomping motions. The girl only smiled and folded her hands.

"This is ridiculous," the monkey muttered, climbing onto the well's edge. "I'll *beep* if I have to. Or invent a new language. Or—"

The monk sat down beside a low wall. Crossed his legs. Watched the leaves.

Time passed.

A breeze came and went.

Even the flies seemed to buzz more softly here.

Then—without fanfare or gesture—a single bell rang out from somewhere unseen.

Low. Pure.

And as if a spell were lifted, the village began to murmur.

Not all at once. Not loud.

But words returned. Carefully.

As if they'd just woken up.

The monk stood. The monkey stared. And the sandal, still broken, made no sound at all.

What truths become clearer when you stop trying to fill the quiet?

PART III
Conversations with A Monkey

GREAT DOUBT, GREAT AWAKENING.
LITTLE DOUBT, LITTLE AWAKENING. NO
DOUBT, NO AWAKENING.

Zen Master Seung Sahn

17

THE MASK WITH NO FACE

They weren't looking for anything in particular.

Just walking. The day was gray in a way that had no mood—neither ominous nor calm. Just... gray.

The monkey tripped over a pile of soggy leaves and cursed.

"Who leaves leaves lying around?" it muttered, kicking at them.

That's when it saw something beneath—half-buried in mulch and mud.

A mask.

Round. Smooth. No eye holes. No mouth. No color. Just a surface that shimmered faintly, like a pond holding still.

"Treasure!" the monkey declared. "Ancient wisdom! Definitely haunted. Or powerful. Or both."

The monk approached, but didn't touch it.

The monkey picked it up. Held it to the light. It reflected nothing.

"No face," the monk said softly.

"Perfect," the monkey grinned. "Try it on."

The monk shook his head. "Why?"

"To see who you really are," the monkey said, now whispering like a stage magician. "Or who you're not."

The monk didn't move.

"Fine, I'll do it," the monkey said, slipping the mask over its own face.

Nothing happened.

Then it gasped.

"I see... someone. Something. A face that looks like mine but... isn't. It's quieter. Older. Less... itchy."

The monk raised an eyebrow. "And how does that feel?"

"Uncomfortable," said the monkey. It pulled the mask off quickly and tossed it back into the leaves. "Too much truth. Not enough flair."
They walked on.

Behind them, the mask lay in the dirt.

The wind picked up. The leaves covered it again—slowly, as if tucking it in.

What might you see if you removed the layers that perform for the world—and are you ready to face it?

18

———

THE DOOR THAT ASKED FIRST

THE PATH WAS WIDE AND EASY, FOR ONCE. SOFT dust beneath their feet, the smell of jasmine drifting in the air. The monkey was humming something off-key. The monk was not correcting it.

Then they saw it.

A door.

No house or walls. Just a freestanding door in the middle of the trail, rooted somehow into the ground, frame and all.

It was painted a faded green. The handle gleamed like it had been polished recently. There were no hinges visible.

"Someone lost their metaphor," the monkey muttered.

They approached.

And just before the monkey could reach for the handle—

A voice.

From the door.

Low, even, unmistakably clear:

"Why do you knock?"

The monkey yelped and jumped back. The monk stepped behind a tree.

They circled it. Tapped the back. Nothing. No puppeteer. No gears. No footprints but their own.

"Did you hear that?" the monkey whispered.

The monk nodded.

"Is it... haunted?"

"I don't know."

The door remained still. Silent.

Then the monkey cleared its throat and tried in its most regal voice:

"I knock... because I seek wisdom."

Nothing.

"I knock because I am humble."

Nothing.

"I knock because—well, because you're blocking the way!"

The door creaked. Groaned. And opened.

Just a sliver.

The monk stepped forward.

The gap didn't widen.

"I think it only opens for one," the monk said.

The monkey frowned. "Unfair."

The monk stood still, then stepped back.

The door closed gently.

The monkey grinned. "See? Patience is a virtue."

The monk walked around the door, stepping off the path and back onto it.

The monkey blinked. "You can do that?"

The monk didn't answer.

**What if the obstacle isn't there to test your worth—
but to remind you of the path you didn't see
beside it?**

19

———

THE TIME THE MONK SAID NO

Tꜰᴇʏ ᴄᴀᴍᴇ ᴛᴏ ᴀɴᴏᴛʜᴇʀ ꜱᴘʟɪᴛ ɪɴ ᴛʜᴇ ʀᴏᴀᴅ, the left path worn and steady, the right overgrown and winding up into unfamiliar hills.

The monkey scratched its chin. "Left is obvious. So let's go right."

The monk paused.

"No," he said.

The monkey stopped mid-step.

"...No?"

The monk turned toward the steadier trail and began walking.

The monkey blinked. "Wait. That's not how this works."

The monk kept walking.

The monkey followed, jogging to catch up. "You always at least *consider* my suggestions. That's the whole dynamic. I tempt, you ponder, then either regret or learn something profound. This is... new."

Still, the monk walked.

The monkey fell into a sulk, trailing a few paces behind.

"No? Just like that? No discussion? No internal struggle? No dramatic pause followed by an ambiguous sigh?"

The monk didn't respond.

They walked in silence for a while.

Then, softly, the monkey chuckled.

"Well, well. Look who found a spine. Or maybe just got tired of circles."

It climbed onto a low branch and swung beside him.

"Let's see where that leads you."

The monk smiled—just barely.

They kept walking.

And behind them, the overgrown path waited, undisturbed.

When you finally say no to your old patterns, what part of you tries to talk you out of it—and do you listen?

20

THE BANANA ARGUMENT

THE MONK AND MONKEY WERE SITTING BENEATH a fig tree, resting after a steep climb.

The monkey reached into the monk's bag and pulled out two bananas.

"Banana time!" it chirped. "Food of champions. Fruit of the free."

It handed one to the monk, then held its own like a relic. With flourish, it pinched the bottom and peeled upward.

The monk peeled his from the top.

The monkey stared. "Really?"

The monk took a bite.

"Of all the teachings, all the lessons, and you still peel from the *stem*?" the monkey said, aghast.

"It opens," the monk replied, chewing.

"Everything opens if you force it," said the monkey. "Doors. Minds. Bananas. But that doesn't mean it's the right place to begin."

The monk took another bite.

The monkey launched into a pacing tirade. "The bottom is gentle. It yields. Peeling from the stem is brute logic— grab the world from the top and bend it to your will. Peeling from the bottom is humility. Patience. Monkey tradition."

The monk raised an eyebrow. "So now bananas are philosophy?"

The monkey nodded solemnly. "Absolutely. The banana is a mirror. How you peel is how you live."

The monk looked at his half-eaten fruit.

"I peel from the top," he said. "Because I don't like over-thinking breakfast."

The monkey snorted. "That's what all tyrants say. First it's breakfast. Then it's borders."

The monk studied his banana. Then, slowly, without a word, tilted his head back and ate the rest of it whole— peel and all.

The monkey froze.

"You... what did you just do?"

The monk wiped his lips with his sleeve.

"I skipped the peeling."

The monkey dropped its own banana. "That's *sacrilege.* You just consumed the metaphor. You devoured the debate."

The monk shrugged. "Or I let go of it."

The monkey staggered backward, clutching its chest. "You've transcended taste. What's next? Biting clouds? Drinking silence?"

The monk stood and dusted off his robe.

Behind him, the monkey fell to its knees and whispered, "Peel from the bottom. It's not too late."

What happens when you drop the argument and simply experience the thing itself?

21

THE SILENT GAME

"You talk too much," the monk said, not unkindly.

The monkey gasped. "I talk *perfectly* much."

"Let's test that."

"With what?"

"Silence."

The monkey stared.

"First one to speak," the monk said, "loses."

The monkey narrowed its eyes. "Fine."

They kept walking.

For seven steps.

Then the monkey's stomach growled—loudly, like a protest from within.

It grabbed its belly and doubled over in pantomimed agony.

The monk kept walking.

The monkey began to mime: first hunger, then thirst, then an elaborate scene involving a dragon, a watermelon, and a broken umbrella. Dust flew. Arms waved. Eyes bulged.

The monk paused once, watching like a museum guest regarding a particularly emotional statue.

Then walked on.

The monkey, now sweating from performance, tried a new tactic. It picked up a stick and began scrawling jokes in the dirt.

Why did the bodhisattva cross the road?

Because the other side was already empty!

The monk didn't look.

Desperate, the monkey did a full-body interpretive dance about longing, regret, and bananas. It ended in a dramatic collapse beneath a thorn bush.

Still, the monk said nothing.

Eventually, the monkey grew tired.

Then bored.

Then, lying on its back, it looked up at the empty sky.

And for the first time since the game began, it wasn't trying to win.

A breeze passed through the grass.

The monk sat beside it.

No one spoke.

And so, the monkey won.

When you stop trying to be heard, what else becomes loud enough to notice?

22

———

THE LIE AGREED UPON

IT WAS JUST BEFORE DUSK WHEN THEY CROSSED paths with the sage.

He stood at the edge of a field, leaning on a crooked staff, eyes the color of things long buried.

He didn't greet them.

Just said:

"Only those who drink rainwater in moonlight will live forever."

Then he turned and walked away.

The monkey snorted. "That's the dumbest thing I've ever heard. Rainwater? In moonlight? What kind of alchemy nonsense—"

The monk tilted his head. "It's poetic."

"It's ridiculous," the monkey snapped. "You can't bottle eternity in a bowl of nighttime drizzle."

91

"Maybe you can," the monk said.

The monkey stopped walking. "You don't *actually* believe that, do you?"

The monk didn't answer.

That night, they camped beneath an old sycamore. The sky was clear. No rain. Only moonlight.

They debated.

"Truth," the monkey insisted, "is measurable. Repeatable. Testable. Like... banana ripeness. Or echoes."

"Sometimes truth is what's useful," the monk replied.

"So lies are fine if they're pretty?"

"No. But some things are true in a way that facts can't measure."

The monkey threw a pebble into the fire. "You're impossible."

In the morning, the sage was gone. No footprints. No trail.

But where he had stood, a flat stone remained—weathered, cracked, and newly carved.

Drink gently.

Under the moon, everything becomes water.

The monkey read it twice.

Then muttered, "Still nonsense."

But it sounded softer this time.

**Have you ever dismissed something as nonsense—
only to feel its truth much later, in a different light?**

23

THE SHADOW THAT BOWED

THEY WERE WALKING ACROSS A RIDGE OF DRY, pale stone, the kind that turns gold in late light.

The sun had begun its slow descent, dragging their shadows long and thin ahead of them.

The monkey was humming. Then stopped.

"Wait."

The monk paused.

"Did you see that?" the monkey asked, voice low. "My shadow just bowed."

The monk looked forward. The monkey's silhouette, stretched across the rocks, did indeed appear slightly bent —arms hanging loose, head lowered. Facing the monk's shadow.

"It *bowed*," the monkey whispered, eyes wide. "Like a monk. Or a mistake."

The monk stood there. Watching.

The wind passed.

They kept walking.

The next evening, they were near the edge of a quiet forest. The sun dipped again, throwing their forms tall and vague across the earth.

The monk's shadow leaned forward now—subtle, but unmistakable—toward the monkey's.

The monkey saw it. Froze.

"Now yours is doing it," it said. "Why?"

Still, the monk couldn't come up with an answer.

They walked in silence for a long time.

Then, without turning, the monkey muttered, "I liked it better when they just followed us."

Do your habits merely follow you, or are they starting to speak back?

24

THE DAY THE MONKEY WAS RIGHT

They didn't plan to find the temple.

It emerged from mist—terraced rooftops draped in ivy, prayer flags shifting with the gentle wind.

Monks moved through the grounds like brushstrokes—each one different: one tall, one hunched, one laughing softly to himself as he swept stone steps already clean. Their rhythms clashed, yet somehow sang in harmony.

"Finally," the monkey said. "A place that understands ceremony."

They were given tea without being asked. No questions. No explanations.

A bell rang once.

In a small courtyard, under a fig tree whose roots tangled like stories, sat the master.

Barefoot. Wrinkled. Still.

His eyes studied them as if reading two lines from the same scroll.

"You've come far," he said. "So I will ask just once."

He held up three fingers.

"One is fire. One is shadow. One is wind. Which burns without leaving ash?"

Before the monk could open his mouth, the monkey leapt forward.

"Wind!" it shouted.

The master nodded. "Correct."

The monkey burst into celebration. It somersaulted. It bowed deeply—twice to the master, once to itself.

"I *knew* it! I *knew* it!" it cried. "I am now Enlightened. Please prepare a robe in gold. And perhaps a title? 'Sage of Invisible Flames' has a nice ring."

The other monks simply watched, their faces serene.

One of them was feeding birds. Another was playing a silent flute.

None said a word.

The master smiled gently. "It shall be arranged."

The monkey ran off to draft his teachings.

The monk lingered, bowl in hand.

The master leaned closer. His voice dropped to a whisper.

"Does he know," he asked, "that you were also correct?"

The monk did not answer.

A breeze moved through the courtyard, shaking one prayer flag—just one.

And beneath the fig tree, nothing burned.

Can a right answer still be incomplete if it comes from the wrong place?

When the mind is nowhere, it is everywhere.

Zen Master Huangbo

25

———

THE ROOM WITH ONE CUSHION

THE PAIR ARRIVED JUST BEFORE TWO.

The sign on the gate read:

"Group Meditation – 2 p.m. – All Welcome."

So they entered.

The room was large—echoes resting in the corners like folded robes.

Thirty cushions were arranged in neat rows, each the same muted color, worn in identical ways.

Except one.

Near the center sat an old cushion, darker than the rest, frayed at the seams.

Someone had sat there long enough to make a dent deep enough for memory to curl up in.

"Where is everyone?" the monkey asked.

The monk shrugged.

The light filtering through the rice paper walls began to change.

They waited.

No one came.

No gong was struck. No master appeared. No others shuffled in to nod and kneel and breathe in rhythm.

Just the sound of wind fussing in the rafters and the faint tick of something inside the monk slowing down.

"Well, this is boring," the monkey said, sprawled across three cushions.

"Group meditation with no group. Classic false advertising."

The monk didn't respond.

The monkey sat up. "You know this is a waste of time, right?"

Still no answer.

The monkey stood. Circled once.

Then twice.

Then muttered, "Fine. I'll go find something that *moves*."

And left.

The monk stayed.

Breath.

A creak.

Stillness.

It wasn't loud.

It wasn't light.

It wasn't bliss.

But something began to fall away.

Not like leaves in wind—more like color fading from old cloth.

A presence that didn't announce itself.

The cushion didn't grow warmer.

The room didn't grow brighter.

But something else did.

And outside, far down the corridor, the monkey sneezed.

Twice.

As if something had just left him.

Have you ever discovered something deeper—not through presence, but through absence?

26

———

THE MONK WHO SLEPT STANDING

THEY MET HIM BENEATH AN ARCHING PINE TREE, where the path narrowed and the air smelled faintly of needles and pride.

He stood as if carved from oath.

Back straight, eyes half-closed, arms at his sides like the breath of a statue.

His robes were sun-bleached and stiff at the seams.

A mat of flattened grass lay beneath him—undisturbed.

"Whoa," the monkey whispered. "Is he... alive?"

The man spoke without turning:

"I do not sit. I do not rest. Not until I am free of all delusion."

"How long's that been?" the monkey asked.

"Twenty years," said the man.

The monkey blinked. "That's a long time to avoid a chair."

The monk bowed slightly. "And have you come closer?"

"Closer, farther—these are illusions too," the man replied.

The monkey rolled its eyes. "Great. He's one of those."

But the monk stepped forward, gently.

"May I ask a question?"

"You may ask three," the man replied.

The monk nodded.

"What is the shape of your delusion?"

The man stirred—just slightly.

"It is wide," he said. "Like sky mistaken for space."

"What keeps it in place?"

"Me," the man answered. "I hold it with both hands. Always."

The monkey snorted. "This is nonsense wrapped in moonlight."

The monk smiled.

Then he asked the final question:

"And what would happen... if you let go?"

The man's eyes closed.

His shoulders lowered.

Something softened.

And for the first time in two decades, he sat.

Not with collapse, but like water returning to its level.

A long breath left him.

Almost a sigh. Almost a prayer.

Then silence.

The monk stood beside him.

The monkey scratched its head. "Did we just win something?"

The man, now seated, opened one eye.

"You may sit too," he whispered.

The monk already had.

What belief or burden have you carried so long that you've forgotten how to set it down?

27

———

THE FOOTPRINTS THAT CHANGED

THE RAIN HAD PASSED IN THE NIGHT, LEAVING the world soft and silver-edged.

They stepped down into a shallow riverbed, the stones slick and the earth still spongey beneath their sandals.

The monk walked carefully.

The monkey bounded ahead, splashing with every step.

Until the monk paused.

He turned to look behind them.

A trail of footprints, deep and even, wound through the mud.

Just one set.

"Strange," the monk said.

"What's strange?" the monkey asked, hopping back toward him.

"There's only one path behind us."

The monkey squinted, then laughed. "Your feet are just heavier. I'm walking beside you, see?"

The monk nodded, though slowly.

They kept walking.

The next day, the riverbed had dried some, but the ground still gave way with each step.

Again, the monk looked behind them.

Again, only his footprints.

The monkey glanced down at its own feet, then at the ground, then back again.

"Huh."

They said nothing more about it.

But that night, as the moon stretched shadows across the earth, the monkey sat by the fire and turned each foot slowly in the light.

Once.

Twice.

As if searching for something that used to be there.

Whose presence have you taken for granted—only to wonder, later, if it had been real at all?

28

THE SOUNDLESS FLUTE

THE MONKEY WAS THE FIRST TO HEAR *NOTHING*.

It tilted its head, ears twitching, tail twitching harder.

"Do you hear that?" it whispered.

The monk paused mid-step. "Hear what?"

"Exactly."

They followed the silence uphill, where a crowd had already formed—farmers with baskets, children clutching rice balls, monks wrapped in indigo cloth.

No chanting. No instruments. No call to gather.

Just a man sitting on a platform, a flute in his hands.

A flute with no holes.

The master lifted it to his lips.

Held a breath.

And played.

No sound.

Not even a whisper of air.

The monkey squinted, waiting for something—anything—to happen.

But the crowd listened, eyes wide and soft, as if they were hearing something they had once forgotten.

Minutes passed.

The master lowered the flute, bowed, and disappeared behind a bamboo screen.

The monkey burst out laughing. "That's it? No notes, no melody, no rhythm. He didn't play a thing!"

One of the children turned to him and said, "He never does."

That evening, the monkey found a hollow reed and attempted his own concert.

He bowed to bushes, blew dramatically, and mimed applause.

The monk said nothing.

After the third attempt, the monkey dropped the reed and muttered, "I think mine was better."

The monk closed his eyes.

"I still hear it," he said.

"Hear what?"

But the monk had already walked off into the trees, the wind parting for him like it had something to say.

What do you hear when there is nothing left to listen to?

読
な
な
DO NOT
READ
NOW NOW
NOW NOW
NOW NOW
NOW NOW
NOW NOW
NOW NOW
NOW NOW
NOW NOW
NOW NOW
NOW NOW
NOW NOW

29

———

THE WRONG SCROLL

THE SCROLL WASN'T HIDDEN.

That was the clever part.

It sat plainly on a low table in the corner of the hermitage library, unguarded but humming with menace.

A single strip of paper hung from its edge, handwritten in red ink:

DO NOT READ.

Naturally, the monkey grabbed it.

"Maybe it's reverse psychology," he whispered. "Maybe it's meant for *me.*"

The monk was already seated in the corner, eyes half-closed, pretending not to notice.

The monkey unrolled the first foot of parchment. Then another. Then another.

Page after page.

No spells. No secrets.

Just one word:

NOW.

Over and over.

Sometimes in tiny calligraphy, sometimes scrawled.

Sometimes upside-down, sometimes mirrored.

"Now," the monkey read.

"Now... now now now now NOW now now now now now now—"

His voice grew frantic, his eyes wide.

"NOW!
NOWNOWNOWNOWNOWNOWNOW—!"

He gasped. His breath caught somewhere between his ribs and his ambition.

Then—

He collapsed backwards onto a straw mat, arms splayed like fallen punctuation.

The monk walked over quietly and rolled up the scroll.

He placed it back on the table, then sat beside the monkey, who lay blinking at the ceiling.

After a long silence, the monkey whispered:

"I've become time itself."

The monk raised an eyebrow.

"I mean," the monkey added, "at least a very loud second."

The monk chuckled.

Outside, a bird called once.

Now.

If every moment is *now*, why do we keep chasing the next one?

30

THE STICK THAT WAITED

A MAGPIE STARTLED THEM FROM THE TREES, then vanished into a thicket of bamboo.

The monkey muttered something about omens and picked a twig from his fur.

The monk just walked on.

But after a few more steps, the monkey stopped.

Stared.

Took one slow turn in place.

"Wait," he said.

The bend in the trail looked ordinary—mossy stones, damp earth, a leaning cypress with bark like peeled paint.

But the monkey's eyes had gone soft, uncertain.

"I know this place," he said.

He wandered off the trail, brushing aside leaves and lifting stones, until he found it.

A crooked stick.

Half-buried, spine bent like a question mark.

Wrapped in moss, but still upright, like it had been waiting for someone to finish the sentence.

"I planted this," the monkey said.

"When?"

"I don't know. Before I knew you. Maybe before I knew *me*."

He knelt beside it.

The monk came closer.

At the stick's tip—barely visible—was a bloom.

Tiny. Pink. Unapologetically alive.

"You planted a walking stick?" the monk asked.

"No," the monkey said. "I *left* it. In a hurry. I thought it was just a stick."

They stood there a while.

Then the monkey whispered, "What else have I left behind that decided to keep growing?"

The monk didn't answer.

But he knelt beside him.

And for once, they didn't keep walking.

What have you left behind that might still be blooming, unnoticed?

31

THE GATE THAT ASKED NOTHING

THE TREES THINNED, AND THE AIR TOOK ON A kind of hush usually reserved for sacred things or deep mistakes.

At the edge of a clearing stood a tall gate carved from blackwood, inlaid with veins of silver and old ash.

Two guards flanked it—one tall, one taller—both still as statues, their robes long like curtains.

The monkey stepped forward first, puffed his chest, gave a respectful nod.

"We're on a very important journey," he said, trying to sound both reverent and in charge. "May we pass?"

One of the guards raised a hand.

"Answer this," he said.

"What is the sound of one hand clapping?""

The monkey lit up.

"Oho! I know this one."

He clapped one hand against his thigh.

He clapped it against his chest.

He waved it in circles like a conductor missing his orchestra.

"No? Not good enough? How about this—"

He smacked a tree trunk.

Snapped his fingers.

Blew raspberries.

The guards did not blink.

"Maybe," the monkey said, panting slightly, "it's a metaphor. For... incompleteness! Or unity! Or loneliness dressed as noise!"

He looked to the monk. "Come on, help me out."

But the monk was quiet.

Then he stepped forward.

He lifted one hand.

Held it in the air.

Let the wind slip through his fingers.

Then slowly, he leaned in and whispered something the monkey couldn't hear.

The gate opened.

Just enough.

The monk walked through.

The monkey stood frozen, mouth ajar.

Then scampered after him.

On the other side, the path curved into shadow.

"What did you say?" the monkey asked.

The monk paused. Looked at his hand. Closed it into a fist.

"I didn't," he said.

**Have you ever mistaken movement for meaning
when stillness was the true key?**

無

32

———

THE TEA THAT WAS ALREADY POURED

THE MASTER WAS FAMOUS FOR ONE THING:

He never stopped pouring.

Visitors came from every province to witness it—students, wanderers, skeptics, thieves disguised as seekers. All left soaked in tea and silence.

So the monk and the monkey came, expecting a mess.

But the cups were already full.

Three of them.

Perfectly still.

No steam, no ceremony.

The master bowed without speaking and gestured for them to sit. The monkey did, cautiously. The monk, with ease.

They waited.

No tea pot appeared. No kettle. No heat.

Instead, the master asked:

"Is the weather in your sandals today?"

The monkey squinted. "You mean dust?"

The master nodded as if this were the deepest truth he'd heard all month.

They spoke for a while about clouds, mud, and the way toes change with long travel.

Then about birds.

Then about nothing at all.

At no point did the tea move.

At no point did the tea matter.

When they stood to leave, the master said simply:

"No tea today."

The monk bowed.

The monkey hesitated, then looked into his cup one last time.

Still full.

Outside, as they descended the temple steps, the monkey muttered under his breath:

"Did we miss the lesson?"

The monk glanced at the sky, then down at his hands.

"I think that was the lesson," he said.

The monkey looked at his own.

And left it at that.

If the cup is already full, what are you still waiting to receive?

33

THE SOUND OF ONE MONKEY

THE MONK WOKE TO A SOFT MORNING—CLOUDS resting low, light bending like it had nowhere to be.

He turned his head, expecting rustling in the trees or a sharp whisper in his ear.

Nothing stirred.

No tail flicking behind a branch.

No humming, no teasing, no familiar chatter.

Just the slow creak of his bones as he sat up.

He waited.

For a voice.

For a complaint.

For laughter disguised as wisdom—or wisdom disguised as laughter.

But the trail was quiet.

Even the wind had forgotten how to interrupt.

He began walking.

There was no hurry.

The hills rose and fell as they always had, though he noticed them more clearly now—the way the grass leaned, the path narrowed.

He passed a river where they once debated fish.

A tree where a mask had once hung.

A bend in the road where a blossom had bloomed from a crooked stick.

Each place greeted him, and he greeted each in return.

By late afternoon, the temple appeared—not grand, but weathered beautifully, like it had been waiting with patience rather than pride.

A master stood at the entrance, sweeping dust from a step that seemed to gather only intention.

He looked up as the monk arrived.

There was recognition in his eyes, though they'd never met.

"Where's the monkey?" the master asked.

The monk looked out over the path behind him.

Then up, briefly, into the trees.

Then down at his own hands.

He smiled.

"Where is he not?" he said.

The master stepped aside. "Then come in."

And the monk did.

Not to find something.

But because he no longer needed to.

What remains when the voice that shaped your journey is no longer there to answer?

Message From The Author

Thank you for taking the time to read *The Sound of One Monkey*. My hope is that these stories have brought you moments of stillness, clarity, or even a small shift in perspective.

This book is part of a larger journey—to share the wisdom of Zen in a simple, accessible way so that more people can experience its teachings and find peace in their lives. In a world that often feels chaotic, even a single story can be a stepping stone to stillness.

If you found value in this book, I'd really appreciate it if you could leave an honest review. Your feedback helps others discover these teachings.

<u>Scan the QR Code or click here to share your thoughts.</u>

Thank you for being part of this journey.

— Kai

References

Kapleau, Philip. *The Three Pillars of Zen: Teaching, Practice, and Enlightenment.* New York: Anchor Books, 1989.

Reps, Paul, and Nyogen Senzaki. *Zen Flesh, Zen Bones: A Collection of Zen and Pre-Zen Writings.* Boston: Tuttle Publishing, 1998.

Shunryu, Suzuki. *Zen Mind, Beginner's Mind.* New York: Shambhala Publications, 2006.

Watts, Alan. *The Way of Zen.* New York: Vintage Books, 1957.

Yamada, Koun. *Zen: The Authentic Gate.* Somerville, MA: Wisdom Publications, 2015.

Mark Morse, trans. *The Gateless Gate: The Classic Book of Zen Koans.* Berkeley: Counterpoint, 2019.

Zen Training: Methods and Philosophy. By Katsuki Sekida. Boston: Shambhala Publications, 2005.

www.ingramcontent.com/pod-product-compliance
Lightning Source LLC
Chambersburg PA
CDIIW021715190726
48289CB00008B/2543